Is It Hanukkah Yet?

**This is how you say
the hard words in this book:**

dreidel: DRAY-dul

Hanukkah: HAH-nuh-kuh

latkes: LOT-kuhs

Maccabee: MAK-uh-bee

menorah: muh-NOR-uh

miracle: MEER-uh-kul

*For Amanda and Ian,
who can't wait for Hanukkah!
—N.K.*

*To Rosie and her Readers
—D.D.-R.*

ISBN 0-439-46963-5

Text copyright © 2000 by Nancy Krulik. Illustrations copyright © 2000 by DyAnne DiSalvo-Ryan. All rights reserved. Published by Scholastic Inc., 557 Broadway, New York, NY 10012, by arrangement with Random House Children's Books, a division of Random House, Inc. SCHOLASTIC and associated logos are trademarks and/or registered trademarks of Scholastic Inc.

12 11 10 9 8 7 6 5 4 3 2 1   2 3 4 5 6 7/0

Printed in the U.S.A.   23

First Scholastic printing, November 2002

Is It Hanukkah Yet?

By Nancy Krulik

Illustrated by DyAnne DiSalvo-Ryan

SCHOLASTIC INC.

New York   Toronto   London   Auckland   Sydney
Mexico City   New Delhi   Hong Kong   Buenos Aires

Today is Hanukkah!
I can't wait to
light the candles
and play games.

"Not yet,"
says Mommy.
"We have to wait
for the sun
to set."

Waiting is hard!
While we wait,
we polish
the menorah.

Hanukkah lasts
for eight nights.
We light one candle
for each night.

Today, I put
two candles
in place.
One candle
is for the
first night of
Hanukkah.
The second candle
lights the first one.

Mommy makes
potato pancakes.
We call them latkes.
I can't wait
to eat one!

"Not yet,"
says Mommy.
"We have to wait
for the sun
to set."

Mommy tells me
the story of the
Hanukkah miracle.
The Maccabees
only had oil
to light their menorah
for one day.
But the oil lasted
for eight days!

Ding-dong.

The doorbell rings.

I run to the door.

It's Grandma
and Grandpa!

It must be Hanukkah now!

"Not yet,"
says Grandma.

"We have to wait
for the sun to set."

Grandpa hands me
a bag of
chocolate coins.
They are called gelt.
"You can eat
these now,"
he says.
I gobble the gelt.

The door opens.

Daddy is home!

I look outside.

It is dark.

"The sun has set!"
I shout.
"Is it Hanukkah
yet?"
Daddy gives me
a great big hug.
"It sure is!"
he says.

No more waiting!

Mommy lights
the candles.
I help say
the prayers.

We play
the dreidel game.
Whee!
All the candy
is for me!

We sing a song
about a dreidel.

Grandma
gives me a gift.

Wow!
It is the music box
we play with
at her house.

"Happy Hanukkah!"
Grandma says.
"Now you can
hear our song
anytime you like."

During supper,
Daddy eats
lots of latkes.
He likes
Hanukkah food.

Do you know
what I like best
about Hanukkah?

Hanukkah lasts
for eight days!
So I get to
do it all again.
I just have to
wait for tomorrow!